The Golden Goose

Dick King-Smith
AR B.L.: 5.0
Points: 1.0   MG

The Golden Goose

Dick King-Smith

The Golden Goose

Illustrated by Ann Kronheimer

Alfred A. Knopf
New York

THIS IS A BORZOI BOOK PUBLISHED BY ALFRED A. KNOPF

Text copyright © 2003 by Fox Busters Ltd.
Illustrations copyright © 2003 by Ann Kronheimer
Jacket illustration copyright © 2005 by Wayne Parmenter

www.randomhouse.com/kids

KNOPF, BORZOI BOOKS, and the colophon are registered trademarks
of Random House, Inc.

Library of Congress Cataloging-in-Publication Data
King-Smith, Dick.
The golden goose / by Dick King-Smith.
p.   cm.
SUMMARY: Farmer Skint and his family on Woebegone Farm have
fallen on hard times, but their luck changes with the arrival of a
special golden goose.
ISBN 0-375-82984-9 (trade) — ISBN 0-375-92984-3 (lib. bdg.)
[1. Geese—Fiction. 2. Luck—Fiction. 3. Farm life—Fiction.]
I. Title.
PZ7.K5893Gr 2005
[Fic]—dc22
2004040842

Printed in the United States of America
March 2005
First American Edition
10 9 8 7 6 5 4 3 2 1

Chapter One

Farmer Skint was a poor unfortunate man.

He was poor because he was not a very good farmer. He always sold things for less than other people did, and he always paid more than other people for whatever he bought.

He was unfortunate because nothing

ever seemed to go right for him. At haymaking or at harvest time, it always seemed to rain. His cows often got foul-in-the-foot, his pigs often got swine fever, and his chickens were always being eaten by foxes.

There came a time when Farmer Skint had lost nearly all his animals. He'd had to sell his remaining cows and pigs and what chickens were left, and all he had now on Woebegone Farm was a pair of geese: a gander called Misery and a goose called Sorrow.

"I'm sorry, Janet," he said to his wife, "but things have got so bad that we shall have to sell the farm."

"Oh no, John, no, John, no!" cried Mrs. Skint. "What shall we do then? The children have to be fed and clothed."

Farmer Skint looked sadly at his two children, a little girl named Jill and a baby boy named Jack. Both looked very hungry. "I don't know about clothes," said the farmer, "but at least we've still got something left to eat."

"What?" asked Mrs. Skint.

"The geese."

"Oh no, John! Not poor Misery and Sorrow!"

"Well, Misery anyway," said Farmer Skint. "Not Sorrow. Not yet. She's sitting on a clutch of eggs. I'll have to let her hatch them out first."

Later that day, he went into his orchard, where there was an old hut. Inside it, Sorrow was sitting on her eggs. Misery the gander was standing guard outside and he cackled angrily at the farmer.

"Sorry, old chap," said Farmer Skint, "but you may be for the chop one of these fine days."

Then he went into the hut and carefully lifted Sorrow off her eggs. She pecked at him furiously, but he was so low-spirited that he took no notice.

But he took notice quickly enough when he peeped in the nest.

He'd had a look the day before and

there had been four eggs, four dirty-white goose eggs, and he was expecting to see a fifth. He was right. There were now five eggs.

But what made Farmer Skint gasp with surprise, what made his heart race and his

breath come quickly, what made his eyes nearly pop out of his head, was the color of that fifth egg. Dirty-white it was not. It was golden.

In the weeks that followed, Sorrow sat steadily upon her five eggs, while Misery mounted guard outside the hut. At nights Farmer Skint shut him inside for fear of the fox.

Then there came a morning when the farmer went into his orchard and was about to open the door of the old hut to let Misery out. But then he thought that the time had come to sacrifice the gander. "At least," he said to himself, "we can have one really good square meal before we all starve," and he made ready to catch up the bird as he undid the bolt on the door.

Yet it was not Misery who came out

first, but Sorrow, and behind her came five newly hatched goslings, and behind them marched their proud father.

Out of the darkness of the hut into the brightness of a lovely May morning they all came, and what he now saw made Farmer Skint catch his breath.

Four of the downy goslings were a pale yellowish color, like most goslings are, but the fifth one was a wonderful bright gold, all over. Even its beak was gold, as were its little webbed feet.

Out of the golden egg, thought Farmer Skint dazedly, has come a golden gosling that will grow into a golden goose!

As the geese stood around him, waiting for the food in the bucket that the farmer was carrying, the golden gosling waddled right up to his feet and stood looking at

him with eyes that were not only bright with intelligence but also golden in color.

Something made poor unfortunate Farmer Skint squat down on his heels and put out a hand and stroke the gosling's golden back. Had he tried to do this to its brothers or sisters, they would surely have

backed away, but the golden gosling stood quite still and even nodded its little head as though it was enjoying his touch.

But more than that, much more than that, as he stroked, Farmer Skint began gradually to feel happier. He looked at his little family of geese and knew, with certainty, that even to feed his own family he could not possibly kill Misery. It was his own misery, he felt, that had suddenly received its death blow.

He looked around his orchard and at his fields beyond and decided he could not possibly sell them. He looked up into the sky and saw what a glorious morning it was, with a sun as golden as his gosling.

Quickly he tipped the food for the geese out of the bucket and ran back to the farmhouse, calling for his wife. When she came out, carrying baby Jack and holding Jill by the hand, she wore a worried face.

"Oh, what is it now, John?" she cried. "What has happened? What has gone wrong?"

"It's Sorrow," he said.

"Oh no, John! Not more bad news?"

But then Mrs. Skint looked more carefully at her husband and saw that he was smiling. It's ages since I saw him smile, she thought. For that matter, it's ages since I did.

"Come along with me, Janet," said Farmer Skint, and he led the way out into the orchard, where Misery and Sorrow were finishing their breakfast while their five children pottered about in the sunshine.

"Now then," said the smiling farmer to

his worried wife, "what d'you think of that, eh?" and he pointed to the golden gosling. "Just look at the color of it!"

Mrs. Skint looked in wonder, and then, letting go of Jill's hand and holding Jack in her other arm, she bent down and stroked that downy golden back. As she did so, the

look of worry gradually left her face and she too began to smile.

Husband and wife looked at one another.

"D'you feel as happy as I do?" asked the farmer.

"Oh yes, John, yes, John, yes! I felt it the moment I touched her."

"Her?"

"Yes. Something tells me it's a little goose, not a gander."

"Well, we'd better think of a name for her," said Farmer Skint. "She may be the daughter of Misery and Sorrow, but she'll have to have a happier name than that."

"How about Joy?" suggested his wife.

"Joy," said Farmer Skint. "That's perfect. Just what we need."

Chapter Two

As they walked back up to the farmhouse,
they met the postman, who had parked his
van by the garden wall and was just about
to walk up the path to the front door.
Instead, he handed the letters to the
farmer.

"Thank you! Thank you very much!"

said Farmer Skint. "It's a beautiful morning, isn't it? Makes you glad to be alive!"

Whatever's come over him? thought
the postman as he drove away. Usually
he's a miserable sort of fellow. In fact, I've
never seen him smile before, but just now
he was grinning like a Cheshire cat.

Farmer Skint ate his breakfast, the letters
lying unopened on the table beside him. It

was his habit not to look at anything the postman might have brought until he'd finished eating. By then he'd feel more able to deal with the post, which consisted mostly of bills.

"A good dish of bacon and eggs for breakfast," Farmer Skint's father used to say, "and a man can face up to anything. Bacon and eggs give a good lining to the stomach."

But now there were no pigs or chickens on Woebegone Farm, so the poor unfortunate farmer had to make do with toast and a scrape of jam. Unfortunate he may have been, and poor, at that moment, he still was, yet he ate his food with gusto. Then he took a paper-knife and slit open the three envelopes that the postman had brought.

The first two contained bills and for a moment his smiles were replaced by a frown, but then he opened the third envelope and the frown vanished, to be replaced by a look of total amazement.

After a while he raised his head and looked around the kitchen table, at baby Jack in his high chair, at little Jill, at his wife.

"Would you *believe* it!" said Farmer Skint in a hoarse whisper.

"Believe what, John?" asked Mrs. Skint, her smile now changing to a frown.

"I've been and gone and won the lottery, that's all," said her husband.

"What d'you mean?"

"Well, years and years ago, when I was a boy, my old dad bought me a lottery ticket. A one-pound ticket it was. It never won anything of course. Till now."

Farmer Skint looked at his wife and his face broke into the biggest smile you can imagine.

"Till now," he said again. "Now it has won something, Janet, that old one-pound ticket has. Guess how much."

"Oh, I don't know, John," said Mrs. Skint. "Ten pounds perhaps?"

"A lot more than that."

"A hundred pounds?"

"Not enough zeroes."

"Oh no, John, don't tell me—you've never won a thousand pounds, have you?"

"No," said Farmer Skint. "This letter is

to say that that old lottery ticket that my old dad bought me has won ten thousand pounds! Look, here's the check." And he waved it in front of his wife.

"Oh, John!" gasped Mrs. Skint in a choked voice. "Our luck has changed at last."

"Looks like it," said the farmer. "We shall have money in the bank again. Or we shall have once I put this check in. There's still a drop of gas left in the old car, so leave the washing-up—we'll all go straight into town."

"And buy some new clothes for the children," Mrs. Skint said.

"And food, all sorts of food, 'specially bacon and eggs. We'll have a second breakfast when we get back."

"And we'll get sweets for the children."

"And gas for the car."

"And new shoes for the children."

"And, Janet, you could have a new washing machine."

"And a new fridge."

"And a new television."

"And toys for the children."

"And it's Market Day tomorrow. I could buy a couple of cows."

"And some hens."

"And a pig or two."

"And perhaps a pet rabbit for the children. Oh, John, everything in the garden is lovely, and you know why, don't you?"

"Yes. I've just won ten thousand pounds."

"Yes, but why have you? What's happened to change you from a poor unfortunate man to a rich and lucky one? Who is the cause of all this luck?"

"It must be Joy," said Farmer Skint.

Chapter Three

What a shopping spree the Skints had that day! As well as buying some of the things they'd talked about, Farmer Skint bought a big sack of corn for the geese and a few sacks of meal and bran that he would mix together to make their daily mash. Misery and Sorrow had been living on rather poor rations recently and they were obviously delighted to be given much more food.

"Kark! Kark!" they cried in their pleasure.

But one morning, after the farmer had given them their breakfast and was eating his own (a good dish of bacon and eggs), he suddenly heard them making quite a different noise—a loud, urgent honking that meant, he knew, that there was danger about. Geese are good watchdogs, which is why the ancient Romans kept them to guard their most important temple. They knew the geese would make a great din if enemies approached.

Farmer Skint was neither ancient nor a Roman, but as soon as he heard the row that Misery and Sorrow were making, he jumped up from the breakfast table. On his way out of the farmhouse, he grabbed his gun, for he had a pretty good idea of what the approaching enemy was.

He was right. Sneaking among the orchard trees was a red bushy-tailed figure.

Misery and Sorrow stood bravely side by side facing the fox, their children grouped behind them. Farmer Skint ducked down behind the low wall of the orchard.

His two geese would, he knew, do their best to protect their family, even at the cost of their own lives, but the goslings would be easy meat for the red raider, who was by now very close.

Long muzzle pointed ahead, eyes fixed upon its intended prey, the fox was poised for a final deadly rush when Farmer Skint fired both barrels.

The alarm cries of the geese now changed to shouts of triumph as the farmer came forward to pick up the limp body of their enemy.

"And d'you know what, Janet?" he said to his wife later. "Misery and Sorrow and four of the goslings just went off down to the pond as though nothing had happened. But the golden one—"

"Joy," said Mrs. Skint.

"Yes, Joy—she stood looking at that old dead fox and then she looked up at me, and it seemed almost as though . . ."

"What?" asked Mrs. Skint.

"As though she was saying thank you."

"Well, you saved her life."

"Thank goodness," said Farmer Skint. "I couldn't bear to lose her."

"I suppose we could shut them all up in the daytime," said Mrs. Skint.

"Shut them up? Where?"

"Well, in the empty cowshed. Then, if another fox comes, they'd be safe."

"But the old ones would be miserable, Janet. You know how they like grazing the orchard grass and swimming in the pond. We'll just have to be on the lookout from now on, or rather on the listen-out, because

Misery and Sorrow will give the alarm if there's any danger in the daytime. I wouldn't worry all that much if it wasn't for Joy."

"Well, put *her* in the cowshed."

"All on her own? No, no. But I don't know what to do. It's a problem."

But that very afternoon the problem was solved. Farmer Skint had just given the geese their midday mash and was standing, watching them eat. He was thinking, as he so often did, how beautiful the golden gosling was. She's safe at night, he thought. If only I could be sure that she'd be safe by day.

As he walked back up to the farmhouse, he had a sudden feeling that he was being followed. He looked round, and there was Joy, pattering along at his heels. He stopped. She stopped. He went on again. She came after him.

Reaching the door of the farmhouse, Farmer Skint opened it and, turning, said to Joy, by way of a joke, "Do come in, won't you?"

She did.

"Oh look, Mummy!" cried little Jill, and she ran forward and began to stroke the gosling's golden back. As she did so, she broke into a huge smile.

Then baby Jack came crawling across the floor and touched Joy. As he did so, he began to chortle with delight.

"Look at them!" said the children's mother. "They love her, don't they? I don't know what we'd do without her now."

"She'd be quite safe in here," said Farmer Skint.

"In here, John?" asked his wife. "Whatever do you mean? You're surely not thinking of having her live in the house? Only dogs and cats live in people's houses. She's a goose. Just think of the messes she'd make."

"I could house-train her, Janet," said Farmer Skint.

"What, to go outside to do her business, like you'd teach a puppy to do?"

"Yes, or better still, we could give her a litter tray, like you would for a kitten. I bet she'd soon learn to use it. Come to think of it, there's an old plastic seed tray in the greenhouse that would do fine. I'll get it now," said the farmer, and he went out. Joy followed him. Before long he came back with the seed tray, in which he'd put a layer of peat. Joy was still following him.

He placed the tray in a corner of the room.

"Now then," he said to the golden gosling, "if you want to do something, you do it in there, okay?"

Mrs. Skint laughed. "Don't be silly, John," she said. "How could the poor little thing possibly understand what you're saying?"

Hardly were the words out of her mouth when Joy waddled over to the seed tray, climbed into it, and did a poo. Somehow neither of the Skints was all that

surprised to see that, instead of the usual dirty-white color that birds' droppings are, these were golden.

"Clever girl!" said Farmer Skint to his gosling, and to his wife, "I bet you she would, didn't I?"

He sat down and looked at his watch. "It would have been time for afternoon milking now," he said, "after I'd fed the pigs and the chickens. But now there are no animals left, so there's no hurry to do anything. I could get used to a life like this, Janet."

"That lottery money's not going to last us forever, you know," his wife said.

"You're right," said her husband. "But then, you never know, Joy might bring us another bit of luck. So shall I put the kettle on? We'll have a cup of tea while I have a look at today's paper."

While Farmer Skint was sitting at the kitchen table, Joy was standing beside his chair, looking up at him.

"She's certainly taken a fancy to you, John," said Mrs. Skint.

The farmer put down a hand and stroked the gosling. Then he opened his newspaper. By chance it fell open at the sports pages, and by chance his gaze fell upon the runners and riders for the afternoon's racing at Ascot.

"Well, would you believe it!" he cried loudly.

"What?" asked Mrs. Skint.

"Look here! Just look at this! I'm not a gambling man, Janet, you know that, but don't you think I ought to have a bet on this one? It's running in the four-thirty— I've just got time to get some money on it." And he pointed at the name of one particular horse.

Chapter Four

"Goodness!" said Mrs. Skint. "You'll have to have a flutter on that, John, won't you!"

Farmer Skint looked at his watch again.

"I'd better get down to the betting shop straight away," he said.

"But, John, your tea?"

"When I get back. It's ten past four

already. I've got to get there before the race starts. I must find my wallet."

Farmer Skint had never been inside a betting shop before and didn't know quite what to do. He went to the counter and said, "Excuse me, I want to put some money on a horse."

The clerk handed him a slip.

"Fill in the horse's name," he said, "and the name of the meeting and the time of the race and the amount of your stake."

"Stake?" said Farmer Skint.

"How much money you're going to bet."

How much money am I going to bet? the farmer asked himself. He took out his wallet, bulging these days thanks to the lottery win. Then he filled in the betting slip.

He took a ten-pound note from the wallet.

"Better hurry, sir," said the clerk.

JOHN'S JOY. Ascot. 4:30. £10

"They're going down to the start now."

But then Farmer Skint suddenly thought, If I'm going to have a gamble, I'll have a real gamble. After all, I'm backing the golden gosling, aren't I? She'll make it come right. He took nine more notes from the wallet and altered the ten pounds to a hundred pounds. The clerk took the betting slip and the money without saying anything, but he couldn't help raising his eyebrows. Whatever's this country bumpkin up to? he thought. Never had a bet in his life before by the look of him, and now he's going to chuck away a hundred pounds on a horse that hasn't got a hope of winning. He looked at the starting prices:

JOHN'S JOY 50–1.

He looked at Farmer Skint and he shook his head sadly.

"They'll be off in a minute, sir," he said, "if you'd care to watch."

"Watch?" said the farmer.

The clerk pointed to the rows of television screens on the walls of the betting shop.

Farmer Skint watched open-mouthed as the runners in the four-thirty at Ascot burst from their starting stalls.

"The early leader," came the voice of the commentator, "is Sweet Thursday by a couple of lengths from Guardian Angel in second, followed by Merry Music. The rest are fairly tightly bunched, with the exception of John's Joy, who is bringing up the rear."

Farmer Skint watched the galloping horses, not knowing the number or the colors of John's Joy, let alone the odds against it winning. But he could see that there was one horse behind all the others. Before he could begin to worry, he heard the commentator saying, "They're coming to the halfway mark now and Sweet Thursday's dropping back. Merry Music takes up the running by a length from Guardian Angel, and the rest are getting a bit strung out as the leader passes the three-furlong post. The early front-runner, Sweet Thursday, has faded and John's Joy is beginning to make good progress through the field. In fact, as they reach the two-furlong post, John's Joy is only a couple of lengths off the lead and going well. Will there be an upset here, I wonder? Is the

outsider going to get into the frame? John's Joy is on Merry Music's shoulder now at the furlong post. Now they're neck and neck—fifty yards to go—it's John's Joy! John's Joy's the winner! It's John's Joy by a length—the outsider's beaten the lot of them!"

She did it! Farmer Skint said to himself. Joy did it! And he went to the counter and handed over his betting slip.

"My horse won," he said. "How much do I get?"

"The starting price," said the clerk in a strained voice, "was fifty to one."

"I'm no good at arithmetic," said Farmer Skint.

"You've won five thousand pounds, sir," said the clerk, and he began counting from a wad of fifty-pound notes.

". . . A hundred . . . a hundred and one . . . a hundred and two," he finished, and handed over the thick packet of notes.

"Wait a minute," said Farmer Skint. "You said I'd won five thousand pounds, but you've given me a hundred and two fifty-pound notes. That makes five thousand, one hundred. You've given me too much."

The clerk sighed.

"No, sir," he said. "Your stake was a hundred pounds—that's what you bet—so, because you won, you get that back.

Five thousand pounds plus one hundred equals five thousand, one hundred."

"So it does," said Farmer Skint. "I'm much obliged." And out of the betting shop he went.

Country bumpkin, my foot! thought the

clerk. He knew what he was doing all right.

Farmer Skint did not go straight back to Woebegone Farm. He went first to a wine merchant's, then to a toyshop, and then to a jeweler's. As nearly as he could (for he was not very good at arithmetic), he spent the hundred pounds that he had staked on a horse— and very much enjoyed doing so.

When he came into the farmhouse laden with parcels, his wife took one look at them and cried, "Oh, John, you must have won!"

"I did," said her husband, "or rather John's Joy did. So I've bought you all presents."

He put the parcels down on the kitchen table and said to his little daughter, "This is for you, Jill." It was a beautiful doll.

Then he said to his baby son, "And this is for you, Jack." It was a big teddy bear.

And to his wife he said, "There are lots of good things in small parcels, Janet," and watched as she undid a very small packet. In it was a pretty necklace.

"Oh, John," she said, "how lovely! Fancy buying all these things for us. You must have won a lot."

"I did."

"Well, you'd better have that cup of tea then."

"No," said Farmer Skint, "I think we'll have something a bit special, to celebrate," and he unwrapped a large bottle of champagne. Mrs. Skint and her

children and the golden gosling all watched as he eased off the cork, and all jumped when it came out with a very loud pop. Then Farmer Skint poured the golden wine into two glasses.

"Cheers, Janet!" he said.

"Cheers, John!" she replied. "My goodness me, you must have won an awful lot of
money to be able to buy all these presents."

"I did," said her husband, and he took
from his wallet that thick wad of fifty-
pound notes and laid it on the table.

"Count those," he said.

Mrs. Skint did so, looking more and
more amazed.

"There's a
hundred of them!"
she said in a dazed
voice.

"Quite right,"
said Farmer Skint.

"That's what I won. Or I suppose I should say, John's Joy won it." And he poured a little champagne into a saucer and set it on the floor before the golden gosling.

"She won't drink that, John!" laughed Mrs. Skint.

"She will," said Farmer Skint.

And she did.

Chapter Five

At first Farmer Skint only allowed Joy to be a house-goose by day. At night he shut her in the old hut with her family. But one evening he thought to himself, she's so good, never makes a mess in the house, always uses her litter tray, doesn't make a noise—she's no trouble at all. I'll let her stay in the kitchen tonight.

After the children had been put to bed and it was beginning to get dark, Mrs. Skint said, "Have you shut the geese up, John?"

"Yes, I have."

"But you've forgotten Joy."

"No, I haven't. I thought she could stop in with us."

"Oh, John, you make a fool of yourself over that bird!"

"Maybe, Janet, but that bird's made a new man of me."

And it was true. Not only was it due to Joy, Farmer Skint thought, that he had won the lottery and the horse-race, but also, he thought, she had somehow changed him from a loser to a winner.

Before May was out, he had bought a

bunch of good-quality heifers, and a couple of well-bred sows, and a flock of handsome young chickens (which he housed in a fox-proof enclosure).

He had not paid more than other people for this livestock, as he once would have done, but less.

And later in the year, when he came to sell his eggs and his piglets and the

occasional bull-calf, he did not sell for less

than other people, as he once would have done, but for more.

That bird has made a new man of him indeed! Mrs. Skint thought now. And a new woman of me, for that matter, and the children love her. It's almost as though I had another child in the house.

"All right, John," she said. "Try keeping her in the kitchen tonight, but mind—any messes, she's out."

"There won't be any," said Farmer Skint.

And there weren't.

So Joy became a full-time house-goose. To be sure, she saw her parents every day, for she always followed the farmer down to the orchard when he went to feed them (he'd sold the other four goslings—for a handsome price, what's more), and Misery and Sorrow were always noisily pleased to see this golden child of theirs.

But Farmer Skint was careful not to take Joy outside unless he was sure there was nobody about. As things were now, he no longer worried too much about foxes, but human thieves would be a different matter. If a dishonest person were to set eyes on his extraordinary bird, she might be stolen.

Really, the only person likely to see Joy was the postman. Nobody else much ever came to the Skints' isolated farm-house. When the new flock of chickens began to lay, Mrs. Skint took the eggs she had for sale to the market in town. She didn't want people knocking on her door.

The postman didn't usually knock, he just shoved mail through the flap of the letter box in the front door—unless he had a parcel too big to go through the flap, in which case he'd press the bell.

One morning toward the end of June, when Farmer Skint was making hay (no rain about now, the weather was glorious and stayed so throughout haymaking and, later, harvest), the postman came to Woebegone Farm with a biggish parcel and pressed the bell. Mrs. Skint didn't hear the ring because she was vacuuming,

but Jill did and went to the front door. She was not tall enough to open it, but just the right height for talking through the flap of the letter box.

"Who is it?" she asked.

"Postman, dear," said the postman. "I've got a parcel for your mummy."

"I can't open the door. I'm not tall enough."

"Well, don't worry, I'll leave it on the step and you'll tell her, will you?"

"All right," said Jill.

"Bye-bye then," said the postman.

"We've got a golden goose," said Jill.

"You've got a what?"

"A golden goose. She's called Joy."

"Fancy!" said the postman. Kids! he thought. They say some funny things. And he got in his van and drove away.

Chance plays a great part in the lives of people, and of geese for that matter.

If the postman hadn't had a parcel to deliver, he wouldn't have rung the bell.

If Mrs. Skint hadn't been vacuuming, she'd have heard it and gone to the door instead of Jill.

If the postman hadn't sounded so nice through the flap, Jill might not have told him about the golden goose.

But the biggest "if" was to do with one of the Skints' nearest neighbors. Not that any of them lived very close to Woebegone Farm, but a couple of miles away there was a large country house that was also on the postman's rounds.

It was called Galapagos House, and it belonged to a famous naturalist and

broadcaster called Sir David Otterbury. And the final strange chance that came about that morning was that when the postman arrived at Galapagos House and knocked on its front door (for here too he had a parcel to deliver), the door was opened by Sir David himself.

The postman knew him of course, as did millions of people who had watched his many television programs about all sorts of animals in all parts of the world, and it struck him that the great man might be amused to be told what the Skints' child had said.

"Good morning, sir. Parcel for you," he said.

"Thank you," replied Sir David Otterbury.

"I heard a funny thing this morning,

sir," said the postman. "You know all about geese, I'm sure."

"I know a bit about them."

"Well, you know the Skints, sir? Woebegone Farm?"

"I don't know them, but I had heard they'd fallen on hard times."

"Oh, their luck's changed," said the postman, "so folks say. But anyway, what I was going to tell you was that I was talking to the Skints' little girl this morning, through their letter flap."

"Through their letter flap?"

"Yes, she's not tall enough to open the door—and you'll never guess what she said to me. She told me they'd got a golden goose. Funny the things kids say, isn't it?"

"A *golden* goose?" said Sir David Otterbury.

"Don't suppose you've ever heard of such a bird, sir?" said the postman. "I thought you'd be amused."

After the postman had driven away, Sir David went to his study to open his parcel and to read the rest of his mail. But all the time, as he was always interested to hear about different beasts and birds, he kept

thinking about what the child had said. A golden goose? No such bird, surely. Yet the phrase rang a bell in his mind. Was it a story he'd heard on his travels? Was it something he'd heard as a child—a fairy story, perhaps? No, don't be so silly, he said to himself. The little girl was talking nonsense or perhaps just talking about one of her toys. Maybe she'd got her birds muddled and it was a golden pheasant that the Skints had. But a golden goose! Rubbish! Still, thought Sir David, I'd quite like to go and have a look and see what bird it is.

Chapter Six

Sir David Otterbury was, of course, a very busy man. He was abroad a good deal, making nature programs in various parts of the world, and even in England he was often away from Galapagos House on business of one sort or another. So it was in fact many months before he was reminded of the postman's story of the little girl who said she had a golden goose.

But then one day he was driving along a country road not too far from his home and there was the signpost for WOEBEGONE FARM. It pointed up a very narrow lane. Ah, thought Sir David, the golden goose! I'll have a peep and see if I can spot this ridiculous bird. I'll pretend I've come to buy some hens' eggs. And he turned up the lane.

Nearing the farmhouse, he saw an orchard with an old hut in it and a pond and a pair of geese, grazing side by side.

Ordinary white geese, thought Sir David. No more golden than I am. Why am I wasting my time? I'll turn round and go back.

But just at that moment Farmer Skint came out of the farmhouse and approached the car.

"Looking for me?" he asked, and then he recognized the face of the driver—a face that he had seen so many times on his television set. The driver smiled at him.

"Good afternoon," he said. "My name's David Otterbury."

"Yes, sir, I know," said the farmer. What's he want? he thought.

"Could you sell me a dozen eggs? I'd be most grateful."

"Certainly," replied Farmer Skint. "I'll fetch them right away."

Thought for a moment he might have heard about Joy, he said to himself as he went to get a tray of eggs. Don't see how he could have, though. But then he suddenly thought how interested Sir David Otterbury would be. Of all the people in the land, he'd be the one who'd be the most interested. Shall I let him see her? thought Farmer Skint. But then he'd tell the world about her, wouldn't he? Not if I swore him to secrecy, though—if I made him promise not to tell.

Farmer Skint still hadn't made his mind up what to do when he came back with the tray of eggs.

"Here you are, sir," he said to Sir David, who had got out of his car and was leaning on the wall of the orchard, looking at Misery and Sorrow.

"Thank you, Mr. Skint," he said.

"You know my name, Sir David?"

"Yes."

"Everybody knows yours," said the farmer. He looked at that pleasant smiling face and made up his mind in a flash.

"You know all about geese, I'm sure," he said.

"I know a bit about them. You've got a handsome pair out there. Have you bred from them?"

"Yes, sir, I have," said Farmer Skint. He took a deep breath. "I'd like to show you what I've bred from them, if you've got a minute."

"Certainly."

"There's just one thing, sir. I don't want anyone else to know. Will you promise not to breathe a word of it to anybody else?"

Don't tell me, thought Sir David, that your little daughter was telling the truth to the postman! Golden goose indeed! It'll just be a brownish sort of bird, I expect. But I would like to see it.

"Certainly, Mr. Skint," he said. "I

promise not to tell a soul."

Farmer Skint went back into the farm-house and a few minutes later came out again, followed by Joy.

Never, for the rest of his life, did Sir David Otterbury forget the thrill of delight he felt at the sight that met his astonished eyes. For walking sedately at the heels of Farmer Skint of Woebegone Farm was a full-grown goose, a goose that was a wonderful bright gold color all over. Even its beak was gold, as were its large webbed feet, and it stared up at him with its golden eyes.

"Ever seen one like this before?" said Farmer Skint.

Sir David Otterbury had, in his time, met many different sorts of geese. Aside from ordinary farmyard geese, he had seen barnacle geese, and Canada geese, and white-fronted, and pink-footed, and lots more. But never had he set eyes on such a goose as this.

"Did I understand you to say, Mr. Skint," he said, "that you had bred this bird?"

"Yes, sir. From Sorrow and Misery out there in the orchard. Sorrow hatched four normal goslings and this one. Give her a stroke, Sir David. She likes that."

The naturalist bent down and ran the palm of his hand gently over the feathers of the golden goose, and as he did so, he began to smile broadly.

"It's a funny thing, Mr. Skint," he said, "but touching this extraordinary bird of yours has made me feel on top of the world! Do you feel she has that effect on you?"

"I do, sir. We all do."

"What is she called?"

"Joy."

"That," said Sir David, "is exactly what I feel."

Chapter Seven

In the weeks that followed, life went on very pleasantly at Woebegone Farm. Farmer Skint's new dairy cattle milked well, his sows gave birth to large litters of piglets, and his hens produced masses of eggs.

However, life at Galapagos House was less serene. Not that Sir David Otterbury was unhappy—how could he be when he had touched the golden goose?—but he was in a worried state of mind. It was very hard to know that this wonderful and unique bird was within a few miles of him and not to be able to tell the world about it. But he couldn't say a word—he had promised Farmer Skint that he would not.

Now that he had seen Joy, he began to feel sure that somewhere, in some book or other, at some time or other, he had once read something about a golden goose. It was an old story, he was sure, that he had come across. He searched through the dozens of bird books in the library of Galapagos House but could find nothing.

Then one night he had a strange dream, and when he woke up he remembered two strange words from this dream.

ANSER AUREUS

Sir David realized, first, that these two words were in Latin and, second, that what they meant in English was GOOSE OF A GOLDEN COLOR.

The Romans! he thought excitedly. That was it, that was what I came across once! The Romans had something to do with a golden goose. And he bolted his breakfast and jumped in his car and raced off to the nearest large public library.

After a great deal of searching through books on Roman stories and legends, he found what he had been looking for.

The Legend of the Golden Goose

During the reign of the Emperor Nero (AD 37–68) there began a belief that one day there would be hatched, from a golden egg, a golden gosling that would grow into a golden goose. This bird would be possessed of magical powers, which would bring happiness, contentment, and good fortune to anyone who touched it. As it grew older, however, the bird, though keeping its magic gifts, would gradually lose its distinctive color. Eventually it would look exactly like an ordinary farmyard goose. At no time during the period of the Roman Empire (27 BC–AD 476) was there ever any report of such a bird, and therefore the legend of the golden goose was gradually forgotten.

"But not by me!" said Sir David to himself. "Those old Romans were right—Joy does have magic powers, I'm sure. But what if they were also right about her losing her color? Somehow I must try to persuade Farmer Skint to release me from my promise, to allow me to show his wonderful bird on television before she becomes as ordinary to look at as Misery and Sorrow. What if she's already begun to change color?"

Hastily he jumped in his car again and whizzed off to Woebegone Farm. He found the farmer mucking out his cowshed.

"Good morning, Mr. Skint," he said.

"John's the name, Sir David," replied Farmer Skint.

"Right," said the great naturalist. "John it is, and you can drop the 'Sir.' I get enough of that. Now then, tell me, how is Joy?"

"She's fine, sir," said Farmer Skint.

Sir David Otterbury held up a finger. "Now, now," he said, "what was I just saying?"

"Oh, sorry, er, David," said the farmer. "She's fine."

"Still that glorious golden color all over, eh?"

"Oh yes. Though there is one funny thing I noticed. Only this morning I saw it."

"Saw what?"

"Well," said John Skint, "I told you, didn't I, that Joy is house-trained? She does her business in a litter tray, like a cat would. But I don't think I told you that her droppings are always gold-colored too. And this morning they weren't. They were just dirty-white, like her mum's and her dad's."

Oh, misery and sorrow! thought Sir David. It's started!

Chapter Eight

It's now or never, said Sir David to himself, and to Farmer Skint he said, "John, my friend, will you do me a great favor?"

"Of course, sir—I mean, of course, David," replied the farmer. "What is it?"

"Will you release me from my promise

to you to say nothing about Joy? Will you allow me to tell two other people—two people I have worked with for many years and would trust to keep the secret of your golden goose?"

"Who are these two people?" John Skint asked.

"One is a cameraman, the other a sound recordist. If you will allow me, I will arrange for them to come here, to Woebegone Farm, and film Joy as soon as possible."

"For the television?"

"Yes."

"But that's the last thing I want," said Farmer Skint. "Why, if you showed her on the television, I'd have the whole world knocking on my door. We'd never have any peace—and what's more, there'd be lots of people wanting to see her, touch her, steal her even. No, no, David, you can't do that to me, not after you promised."

"Hang on a minute, John," said Sir David Otterbury. "There's something you don't know about. Hear me out while I make you another promise, which is—I will not show any film of your golden goose as long as she is still golden."

"Whatever do you mean? She always will be."

"She may not," said Sir David, and he told the farmer about the Roman legend.

"She may change, you see," he said. "Today her droppings are no longer gold. Tomorrow—next week, next month, who knows—it may be her feet or her beak or her eyes that lose their color, and then her feathers, until she is a golden goose no longer. But, John, if only you will allow me to film her now, then we will have a record of her for all time. I promise not to show the film on television till she's lost all her color."

"And if she doesn't?"

"Then I won't show it at all. I'll keep it as a private record of her, just for your family and for me."

Suppose those old Romans were right? Farmer Skint thought. Suppose that before long Joy will be golden no more? It would be dreadful not to have a picture of his beautiful golden goose.

"All right, David," he said at last. "You go ahead. I trust you."

"Thank you, John," said Sir David Otterbury. "And just remember that if a film of Joy is ever shown on television, they'll pay a great deal of money for it and I'll make sure a large part of it comes to you."

Sir David worked fast. Two days later he was out in the orchard at Woebegone Farm with his cameraman and sound recordist, giving a commentary as Joy walked down to the pond between her proud white parents, and the three of them swam together in the morning sunshine.

"Never," he said, "has such a bird as this been seen before. Golden from top to toe—feathers, eyes, beak, feet—this goose is a creature hitherto unknown to science, and is certainly the most amazing discovery of my life as a naturalist. The only reference to it was made by the ancient Romans nearly two thousand years ago,

some of whom believed in the magic powers of the bird they called 'Anser Aureus,' the Golden Goose. To touch it, they said, was to experience instant happiness."

No sooner had he finished speaking into the microphone than Joy left Misery and Sorrow floating on the sunlit water. She walked up out of the pond and waddled straight toward the camera and stopped and stood, waiting. And Sir

David Otterbury stepped into the shot and bent and stroked her golden back.

Then he straightened up and turned to the camera, his face wreathed in smiles.

"The Romans were right!" he said.

Chapter Nine

As they drove away from Woebegone Farm, the cameraman said to the sound recordist, "What a bird, eh?"

"Never seen anything like it," replied the other, "and nor has the old Otter either. Never seen him so pleased. I mean, when we were filming those mountain gorillas, years ago, remember? And they were crawling all over him and he was looking as though he loved it? But today he looked even happier."

"Yes," agreed the cameraman. "I got some lovely shots."

"And I got some good wild track too," said the sound recordist. "Cows mooing,

birds singing, and those two old white geese honking away—to show how proud they were of their daughter, I suppose."

"Someone's going to pay a great deal of money to show this little bit of film we've just made."

"Pity it has to be a secret," said the sound recordist, "but when the old Otter tells me to keep mum, I keep mum."

Sir David Otterbury, meanwhile, had gone back to Galapagos House. Before he left, he said to Farmer Skint, "Now, John, as soon as that bit of film is processed and edited, you must all come over to my place and see it."

"See it? On the television, you mean? But you promised you wouldn't show it while she's still golden!"

"No, not on the television. I've got my

own little projection room at Galapagos House—a kind of mini-cinema. I'll show you the film there when it's ready. Now please will you promise me something, John, before I go?"

"What?"

"Promise to let me know when there's any further loss of color from your wonderful golden goose."

"You think there's bound to be, do you, David?"

"I've a nasty feeling that those old Romans were right. But try not to worry too much, John. They also said that such a bird would still retain its magic gifts."

A week later the phone rang in Galapagos House.

"Hullo, David Otterbury here."

"It's John Skint."

"John, what news?"

"The Romans were right. The color has nearly gone from her webs and her beak and her eyes."

"What about her plumage?"

"Not as bright as it was."

"Thank goodness I persuaded him to let me make that film!" said Sir David to himself as he put the phone down. "Looks like we were only just in time."

A couple of weeks later two things happened: the film of Joy, the golden goose, arrived at Galapagos House, and at Woebegone Farm Joy was golden no longer.

Sir David came over the next day and they all went out into the orchard together, he and John Skint and Janet Skint and Jill Skint and Jack Skint (who was toddling by now). They stood looking at not two but three ordinary white geese.

"Which is Joy?" asked Jill.

"Joy gone?" asked Jack.

"No," said Farmer Skint. "She hasn't gone. She's just changed color, that's all. She's still our lucky magic goose." And he called, "Come, Joy!" and one of the three white geese waddled forward and stood before them, and each of them in turn stroked the feathers of her back, feathers that had been brilliant gold and were now dull white.

But all of them, from the oldest to the youngest, felt a thrill of happiness and contentment as they stroked, and little Jack summed the whole thing up.

"Joy not gone!" he said happily.

That afternoon the Skints all went over to Galapagos House to see the film. The voice-over, the camera work, the sound were all perfect, and no one in the world,

seeing the shots of Joy, would ever be able to doubt that there was such a bird as a golden goose.

After tea—with hot buttered crumpets for John and Janet and chocolate-chip ice cream for Jill and Jack—Sir David Otterbury said to Farmer Skint, "Now then, John, what are we going to do? Are we going to keep this film to ourselves, or are we going to show the golden goose to the world?"

John Skint turned to his wife. "What do you think, Janet?"

"I think," said Janet Skint, "that Sir David would be very disappointed if he couldn't show the film on television. And it would be lovely for other people and their children to see our Joy as she used to be. After all, no one can bother us about it—we haven't got a golden goose anymore. But just think how interested thousands of other people would be to see her."

"Millions," said Sir David. "And as I told your husband, Mrs. Skint, the television companies will fight tooth and nail for the rights to screen this film. They will pay a great deal of money for it, I've no doubt, and I will pay John a very fair share of it."

That goose, thought Janet Skint—she always earns us money, one way or another.

"I'm happy about it, John," she said to her husband, "if you are."

"I am," said John Skint.

"And so am I," said Jill Skint.

As for Jack Skint, it was all a bit confusing for him, but he was very happy because of what he'd just seen.

"Joy gold again!" he said.

Chapter Ten

When that film of the golden goose was shown on television—not just British television but all over the world—it created an enormous sensation. Sir David Otterbury received a huge amount of praise (and indeed a huge amount of money, a very fair share of which went, as had been promised, into Farmer Skint's pockets).

The cameraman and the sound recordist did very nicely out of it too.

"Let's just hope," one said to the other, "that the Skints won't have to put up with masses of people coming to Woebegone Farm to have a look at the bird."

But he needn't have worried. True, there were newspaper reporters who snooped around a number of farms near Galapagos House, but though Farmer

Skint did, they could see, have geese, they were very ordinary ones.

One person who saw the film on TV and was puzzled was the postman.

"Funny, you know," he said to his wife, "but about a year ago, at Woebegone Farm, the farmer's little daughter told me they had a golden goose and I mentioned it to Sir David Otterbury and I could swear that orchard in the film was Farmer Skint's orchard. But I was there delivering mail only yesterday and his geese are ordinary white ones. I tell you what I've just realized—the whole thing was a con! They painted one of those geese with gold paint! What a spoof! I'd never have believed Otterbury was so deceitful!"

For Farmer Skint, who had once been a poor unfortunate man, things were going swimmingly.

True, when he cleaned out Joy's litter tray, he still nurtured a dim hope that perhaps her droppings would turn gold again, but they never did, and in time the Skints decided that, though Joy would always be welcome in the farmhouse, it was now time that she had a home of her own and, what's more, a husband.

So with some of the money he'd got from the film, John Skint bought a brand-new wooden shed. Joy obviously thought it was beautiful, but Misery and Sorrow were too old for change and preferred their original hut.

He then bought a handsome young gander (whom Joy also thought beautiful), a jolly sort of fellow they named Merriment. Misery was none too keen on having another gander about the place, but Merriment was polite to him and kept out of his way, and the young couple slept happily in the new shed.

One morning the following spring, Farmer Skint finished the milking and then, before feeding his pigs and his chickens and going for his own breakfast, he went out into the orchard and opened the door of the old hut to let out Misery and Sorrow. Then he went to the new shed to let out Joy and Merriment. Then something made him look inside it.

After he'd had his breakfast (bacon and eggs, a good lining to the stomach), he said to his wife, "Guess what, Janet."

"What?"

"Joy has laid her first egg."

"Oh, that's wonderful!" she cried.

"It is indeed wonderful," said Farmer Skint. "Guess what, Janet."

"What?"

"It's a golden egg."

ABOUT THE AUTHOR

DICK KING-SMITH was born and raised in Gloucestershire, England. He served in the Grenadier Guards during World War II, then returned home to Gloucestershire to realize his lifelong ambition of farming. After twenty years as a farmer, he turned to teaching and then to writing the children's books that have earned him many fans on both sides of the Atlantic. Inspiration for his writing comes from his farm and his animals.

Among his well-loved novels are *Babe: The Gallant Pig*, *Harry's Mad*, *Martin's Mice* (each an American Library Association Notable Book), *Ace: The Very Important Pig* (a *School Library Journal* Best Book of the Year), *Three Terrible Trins*, *The Stray*, *A Mouse Called Wolf*, *Titus Rules!*, *Funny Frank*, and his memoir, *Chewing the Cud*. Additional honors and awards he has received include a *Boston Globe–Horn Book* Award (for *Babe:*

The Gallant Pig) and the California Young Reader Medal (for *Harry's Mad*). In 1992 he was named Children's Author of the Year at the British Book Awards. In 1995 *Babe: The Gallant Pig* became a critically acclaimed major motion picture.